KT-394-255

This is a
cat.

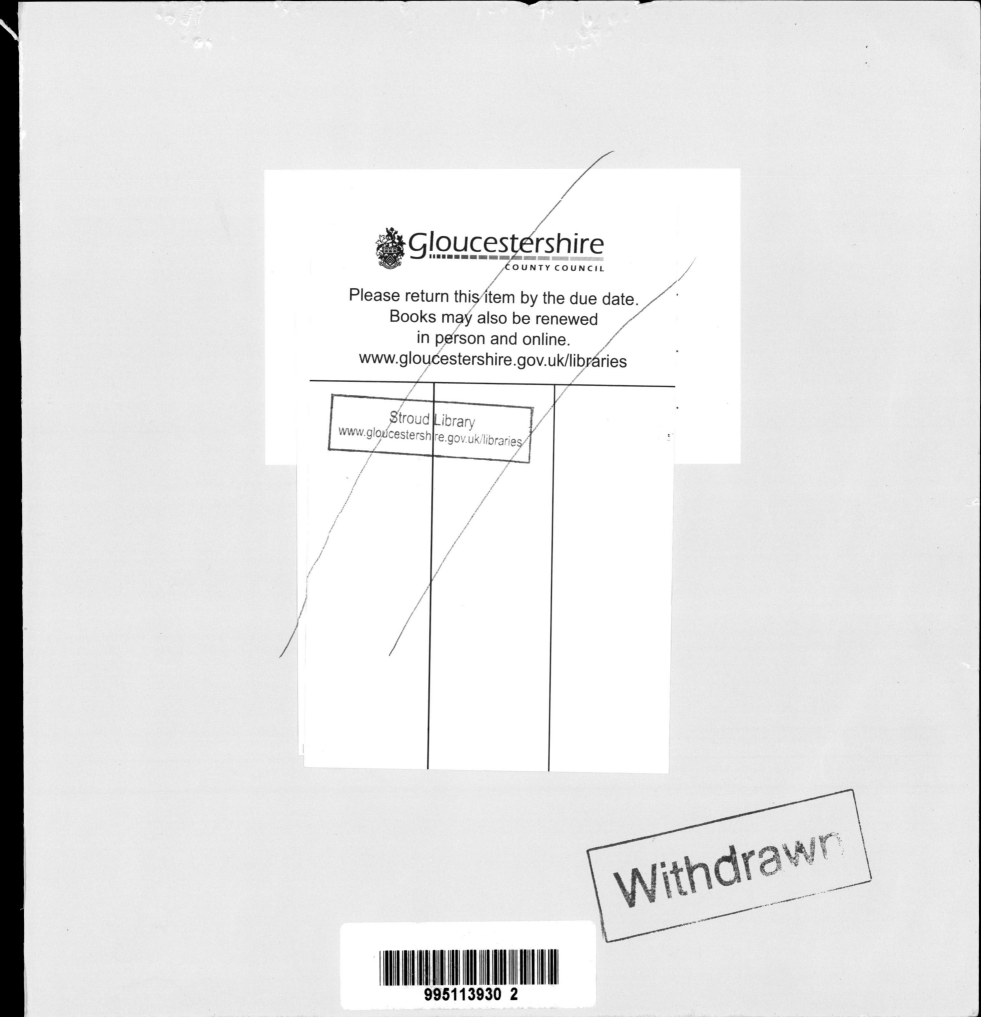

Gloucestershire
COUNTY COUNCIL

Please return this item by the due date.
Books may also be renewed
in person and online.
www.gloucestershire.gov.uk/libraries

Stroud Library
www.gloucestershire.gov.uk/libraries

Withdrawn

995113930 2

For my dog, Hugo.
Who taught me the meaning of irony
by destroying some of the artwork
from this book.

First published 2019 by Nosy Crow Ltd
The Crow's Nest, 14 Baden Place, Crosby Row
London SE1 1YW
www.nosycrow.com

This edition published 2020

ISBN 978 1 78800 515 9 (HB)
ISBN 978 1 78800 922 5 (PB)

Nosy Crow and associated logos are trademarks and/or
registered trademarks of Nosy Crow Ltd.

Text and illustrations copyright © Ross Collins 2019
The right of Ross Collins to be identified as the author
and illustrator of this work has been asserted.
All rights reserved.

This book is sold subject to the condition that it shall not, by way of trade or otherwise,
be lent, hired out or otherwise circulated in any form of binding or cover other than
that in which it is published. No part of this publication may be reproduced, stored
in a retrieval system, or transmitted in any form or by any means (electronic, mechanical,
photocopying, recording or otherwise) without the prior written permission of Nosy Crow Ltd.

A CIP catalogue record for this book is available from the British Library.

Printed in China
Papers used by Nosy Crow are made from wood grown in sustainable forests.

No animals were harmed in the making of this book but plenty of them were really annoyed.

1 3 5 7 9 8 6 4 2 (HB)
1 3 5 7 9 8 6 4 2 (PB)

~~My First Animal Book~~

This is a Dog

~~ROSS COLLINS~~ by a dog

nosy crow

This is a
dog.

This is a
monkey.

This is a
rabbit.

This is a
squirrel.

This is a
~~crocodile.~~

dog

This is a
giraffe.

This is an
elephant.

This is a
bear.

This is a

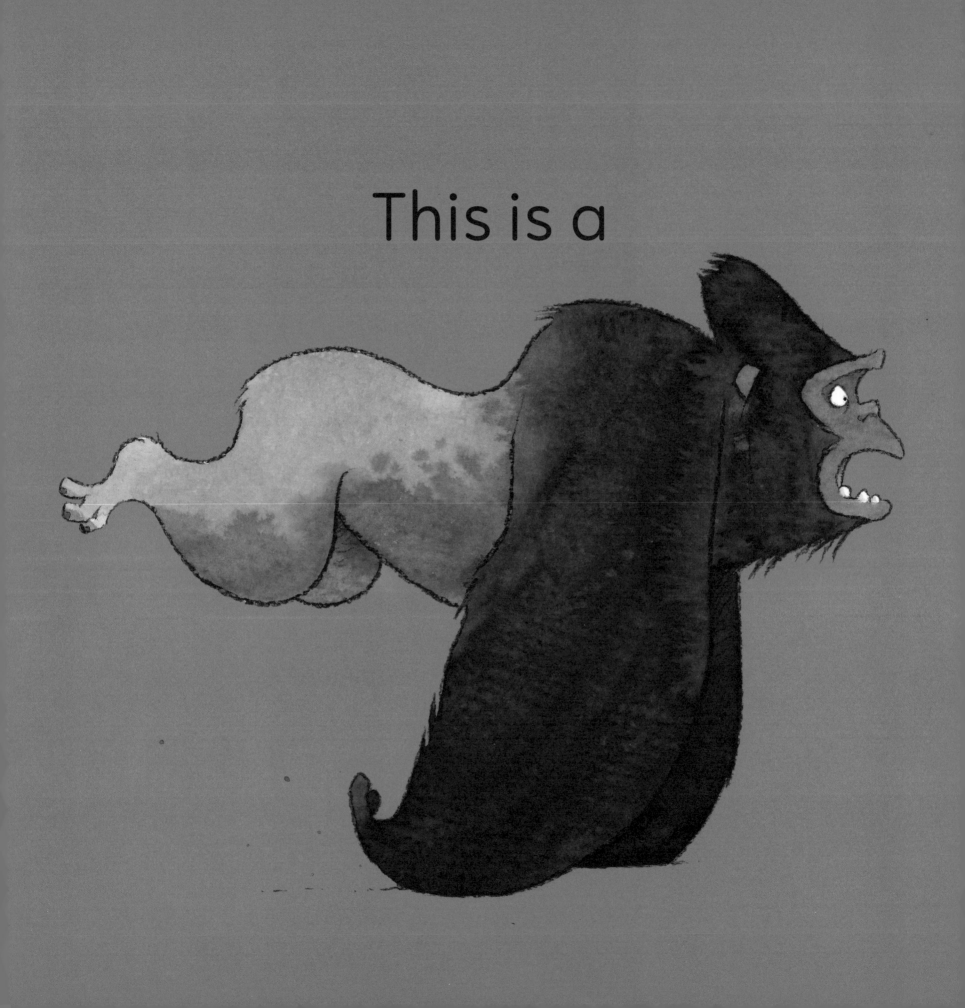

gorilla.

This is a
chase.

This is a
trick.

This is
~~the end.~~
a dog!